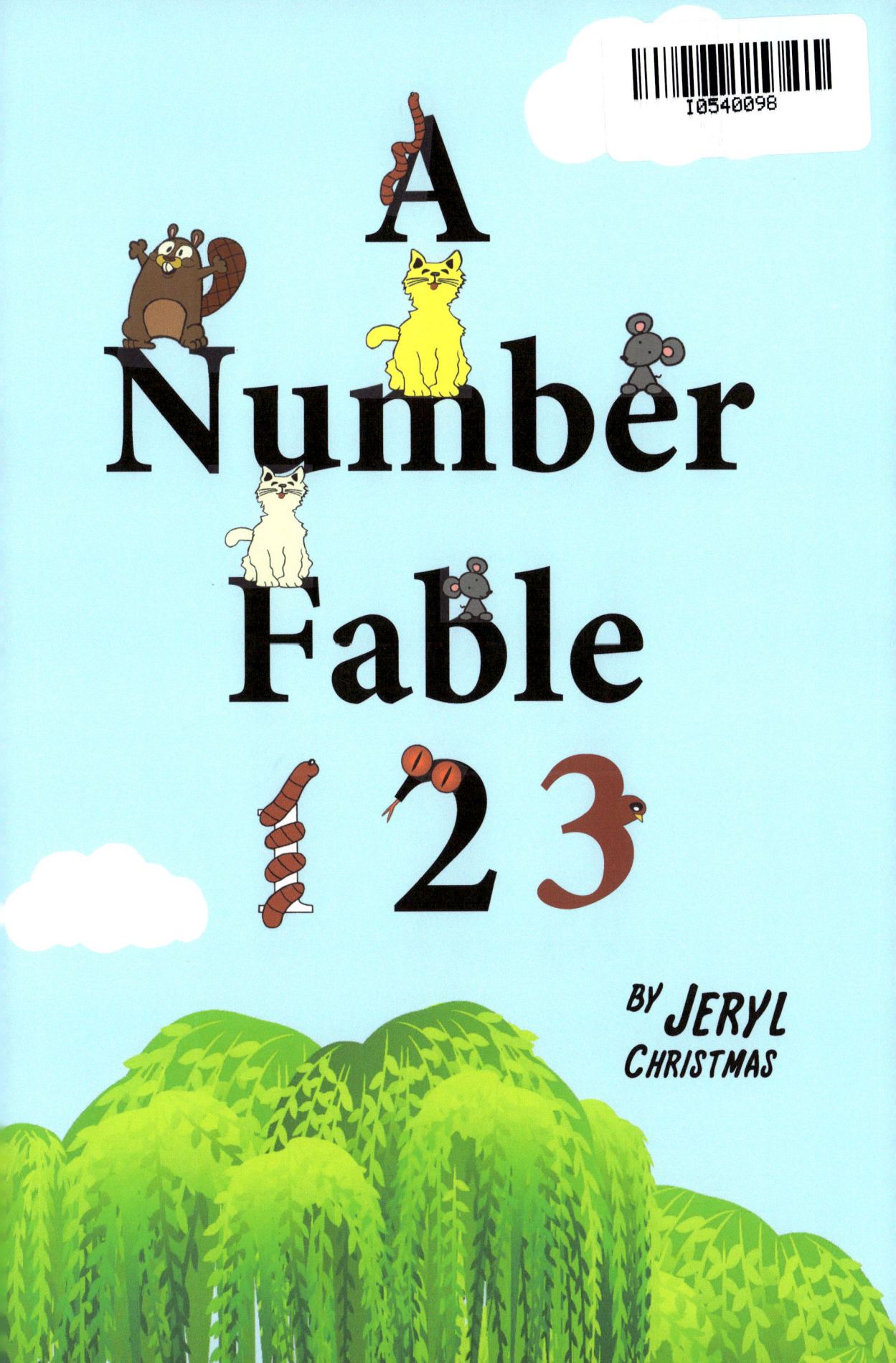

A Number Fable 123

BY JERYL CHRISTMAS

This Book Belongs To

_____

This book is dedicated to my
great nephew, Parks, an avid lover
of books and animals.

1 ONE

ONE wiggly worm went
wandering one day
way up in a
weeping willow tree.

And what did he see
from the canopy?
"A world," he said,
"especially for me."

2 TWO

Then to his surprise
he saw **TWO** twinkling eyes
from a towering, testy snake
from overhead.

The two looked around
from such a distance to the ground.
"Take a look at all the others,"
they both said.

3 THREE

For through the thrilling sky,
THREE thrushes fluttered by,
so the twosome knew that they
were not alone.

The wondrous world they saw
was filled with one and all.
"Let's unite and work together
from now on."

4 FOUR

Then **FOUR** furry felines
sitting on some tree vines
figured they would get
into the act.

They knew that they could stand
to lend a helping hand,
so the four decided they would
make a pact.

5 FIVE

They'd try to give advice
to all **FIVE** of the mice
that lived below along
a winding trail.

"Don't ever tease the cats
if they're hunting mice or rats.
Just be still and very quiet
for a spell."

6 SIX

On another trail were **SIX**
of some very sturdy sticks,
so a beaver moseyed over
to explore.

These sticks would build his home
with no further need to roam
if only there were help
to do the chore.

7 SEVEN

The help came in **SEVEN**s
like lights from the heavens.
The cry was heard for peace
and harmony.

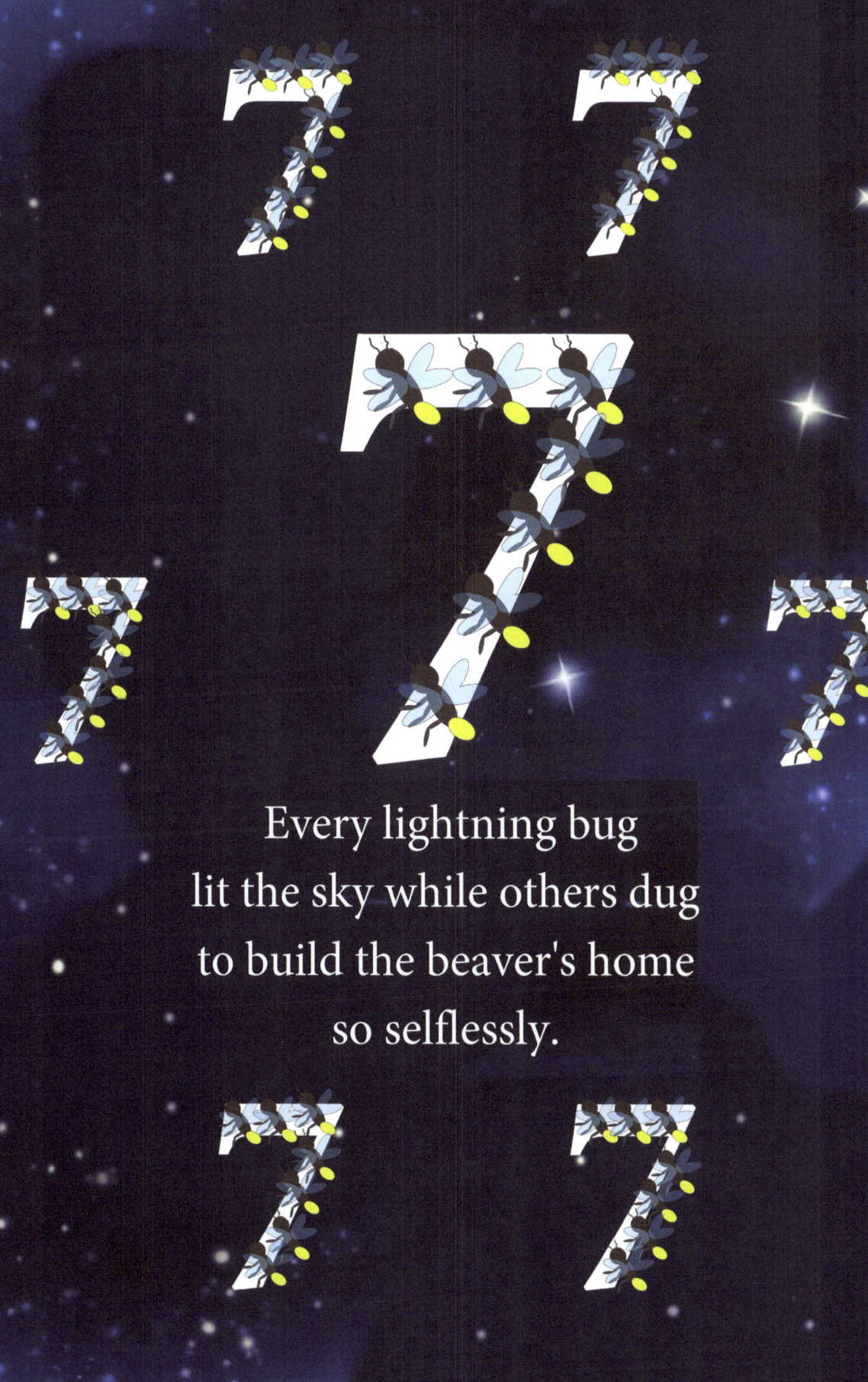

Every lightning bug
lit the sky while others dug
to build the beaver's home
so selflessly.

8 EIGHT

Now things were going great,
but down below there were EIGHT
of the hungriest, pesty critters
known to man.

The termites crawled around
two circles underground.
To eat the beaver's home
was now their plan.

9 NINE

But termite number NINE
thought it wrong for them to dine
on their neighbor's home,
and so she left the team.

Now filled with new-found love,
she made her way above
to confess to others of her brothers'
scheme.

10 TEN

Then **TEN** gathered 'round
leaving bullies underground,
and the worm addressed
the circle of them all.

The termite got applause
for taking up the cause
of adding peace and love
into their law.

The moral of this tale,
and it shall never fail,
is work together
always being kind.

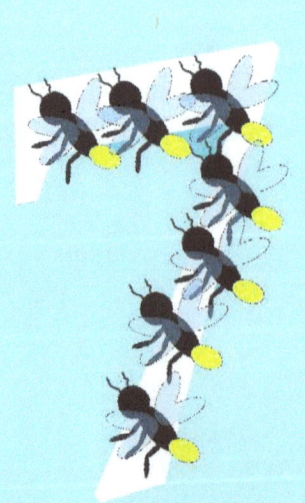 

If we all do our part,
each following his heart,
then peace and love
will be the ties that bind.